Goodnight My Sweet Violet

Heather Young

Dedicated to my sweet Vylett Jai
without whom my days would be very dull. I love you.

My favorite part of the day,
is not the morning's sunshine rays
It's after you've woken up with a frown
'cause your favorite dolly can't be found

It's after you eat your egg and waffle
only to tell me they taste so awful.
It's after your bath as you holler and shout,
you don't want to get in nor want to get out.

It's after the fuss when I comb your hair
it's after you can't decide what to wear.

It's after fighting your brother when you don't want to share.

Then it is already lunchtime, just how can that be?
You want peanut butter but I made macaroni.
You mumble and grumble you won't take a bite.
It's only twelve noon and we're on our 3rd fight.

It's time to play outside we have so much fun.
We play hopscotch under the bright warm sun.
You give me a kiss and I give you one too,
then I remember how much I love you.
But that's still not my favorite part of the day
it is still yet to come, it is not far away.

Daddy is home now; he has worked long and hard
He's ready to hear what you've done to the yard.
You picked all my flowers, the pretty bright blooms,
So I sigh and stomp and I frown with a gloom.

Then you give me a pink one with a big grin
How can I be mad? You melt my heart again.

It's dinnertime- you bow your head to say a prayer
you thank the Lord for all His love and tender care.
Your words touch my heart and bring a tear to my eye
you are the sweetest girl and I could almost cry.
We eat and we laugh and then we are done
But my favorite part is still to come.

The dishes are done; the toys put away,
there is not much left in our fun-filled day.
You choose a bedtime story, your favorite book
we snuggle in close as you give a sleepy look.
My favorite part of the day
is just a moment away!

It's when you softly whisper, "Mommy I love you."
It's when I whisper back, "I am so glad you do."
As I bend down to softly kiss your cheek
I turn out the light and begin to think...
How much I'd miss the fighting, the quarrels and even the tears
If you had not been with me for the last 3 ½ years.

As I walk away I look back to say,
"Goodnight my Sweet Violet, you're my favorite part of the day!"

Made in the USA
Lexington, KY
14 November 2011